The Classic Treasury of
GRIMM'S FAIRY TALES

The Classic Treasury of

GRIMM'S FAIRY TALES

Illustrated by Don Daily

Retold by Danielle McCole

COURAGE
BOOKS

AN IMPRINT OF RUNNING PRESS
PHILADELPHIA · LONDON

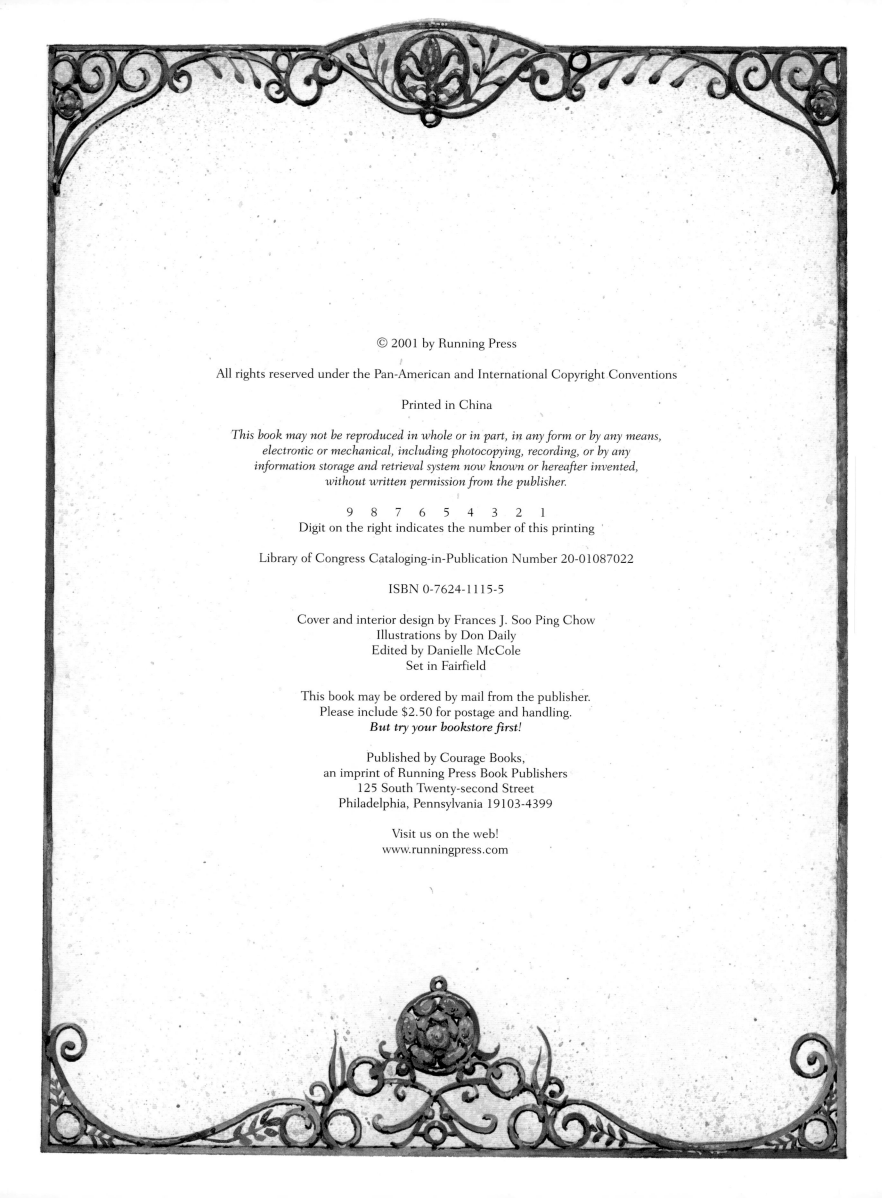

9 8 7 6 5 4 3 2 1
Digit on the right indicates the number of this printing

Library of Congress Cataloging-in-Publication Number 20-01087022

ISBN 0-7624-1115-5

Cover and interior design by Frances J. Soo Ping Chow
Illustrations by Don Daily
Edited by Danielle McCole
Set in Fairfield

This book may be ordered by mail from the publisher.
Please include $2.50 for postage and handling.
But try your bookstore first!

Published by Courage Books,
an imprint of Running Press Book Publishers
125 South Twenty-second Street
Philadelphia, Pennsylvania 19103-4399

Visit us on the web!
www.runningpress.com

To my two wonderful witches Deborah Levine

and my wife Renée, my Hansel and Gretel

Conor Foote and Laura Levine, my prince Steve Gilhool,

and last but not least my lovely princess,

my daughter Susie.

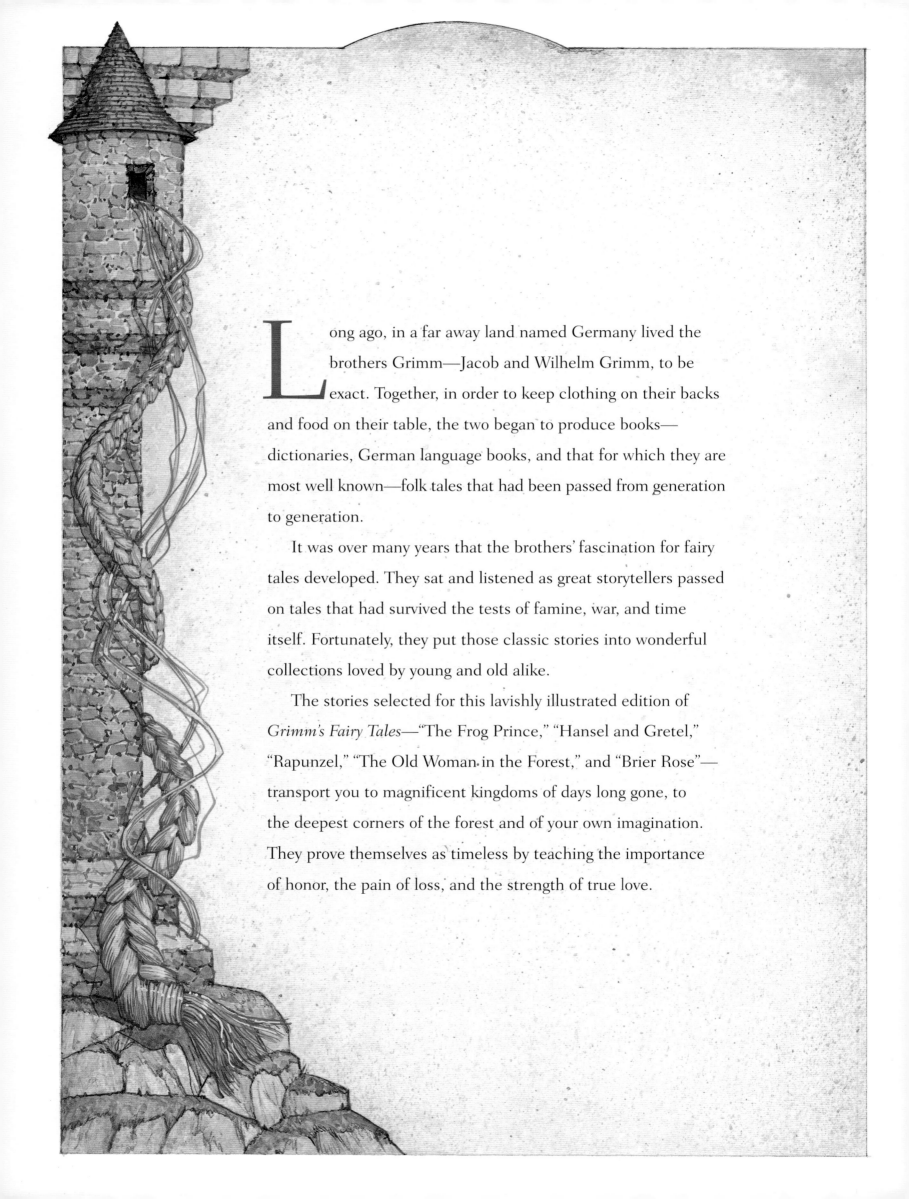

Long ago, in a far away land named Germany lived the brothers Grimm—Jacob and Wilhelm Grimm, to be exact. Together, in order to keep clothing on their backs and food on their table, the two began to produce books— dictionaries, German language books, and that for which they are most well known—folk tales that had been passed from generation to generation.

It was over many years that the brothers' fascination for fairy tales developed. They sat and listened as great storytellers passed on tales that had survived the tests of famine, war, and time itself. Fortunately, they put those classic stories into wonderful collections loved by young and old alike.

The stories selected for this lavishly illustrated edition of *Grimm's Fairy Tales*—"The Frog Prince," "Hansel and Gretel," "Rapunzel," "The Old Woman in the Forest," and "Brier Rose"— transport you to magnificent kingdoms of days long gone, to the deepest corners of the forest and of your own imagination. They prove themselves as timeless by teaching the importance of honor, the pain of loss, and the strength of true love.

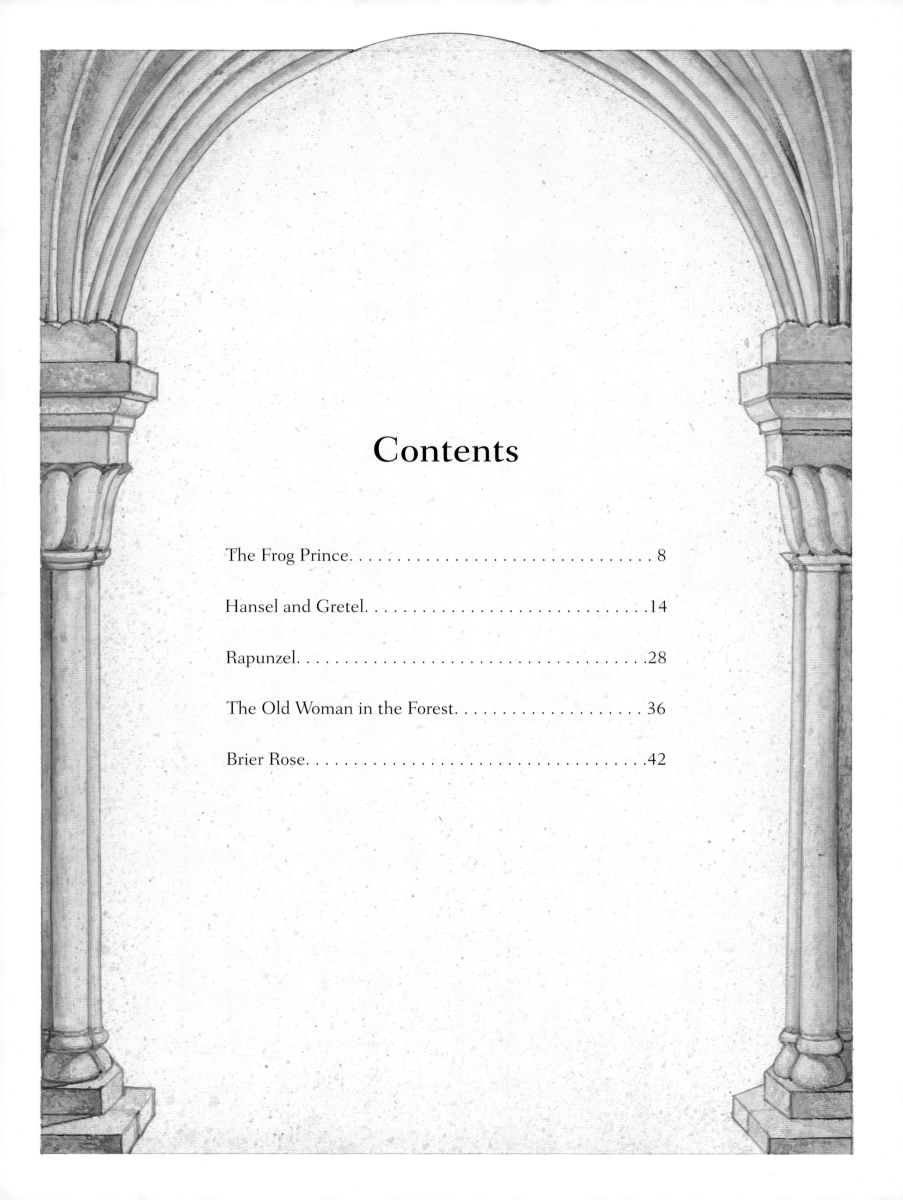

Contents

The Frog Prince

Long ago, in a far away place, there lived a king and his beautiful daughter. On days when the palace became too hot, the princess would visit a little well that was nestled within the nearby forest. There she would enjoy the protection of the shade and the cool of the water as she played with her favorite golden ball. She would throw the ball into the air and catch it in her delicate little hands. But one time she did not catch the ball and it splashed into the water of the well.

The princess gazed into the darkness of the well, sure that her beloved ball was lost forever, and she sat and cried.

From behind her came a small voice asking, "What is it that has made you cry, little princess?"

As she cleared the tears from her eyes, the princess turned to find a frog, peeking at her from a puddle.

"My golden ball has fallen into the well and I have no way to get it back."

"Please, stop your crying, princess. I will retrieve the ball for you."

"Oh, thank you so much, little frog!" The princess said with great joy.

"All that I ask in return is that you promise that you will give me a kiss in return."

"Oh! Of course! Yes, please just get the ball," said the princess. But little did the frog know that she was thinking, *That ugly frog will never have a kiss from me. I am a beautiful princess and he is only a lowly frog.*

Trusting in the promise of the princess, the frog leapt into the well and before long, had returned to the surface with the princess's ball.

The princess was so pleased to

have her ball back that she ran off happily, back to the kingdom, without even thanking the frog.

The following evening, as the princess sat down to dinner with her father, they heard a rapping on the door.

A small voice, just beyond the door, called out, "Princess, please come and open the door!"

The princess went to the door only to find the same little frog from the well, sitting on the front step.

"Who is it at the door, my dear?" asked the king.

"It's an awful, disgusting frog, " answered the princess.

When the king asked the princess why the frog had come to their palace, the princess told him the whole story of the promise that she had made to him the previous night.

"I never imagined that I would have to keep my promise. Look at him, father! He is just a lowly frog."

"You have given your word, and you must keep it," said the king.

"I am here for the kiss that you promised me."

The princess squirmed at the thought of kissing the ugly little frog. But her father glared at her and she knew that she must go through with it. She lifted the frog to her face and as she looked at him she noticed something beautiful and sweet in his eyes. She kissed him quickly and returned him to his place on the ground.

Before the princess knew what was happening, the ugly little frog changed right before her into a handsome prince—a prince with the same beautiful eyes that the frog had.

"Finally the spell has been broken," cried the prince. He stared at his fingers and hands with absolute joy. "I was put under the spell of an evil enchantress many, many years ago, and nothing could free me from its grip, but the kiss of a fair princess. You have saved me!"

The princess stood there, ashamed of how she had behaved. "I am so very sorry. Can you ever forgive me for how I treated you?"

"Why, yes, princess. Of course I can. But you must promise that you will always keep your word. You see, all things are not always as they seem."

A wide smile spread across the face of the princess as she said, "I will always remember that. I promise."

And so, they lived happily ever after.

Hansel and Gretel

There was once a young boy and girl that lived at the edge of a great, dark forest with their loving father, a woodcutter, and evil stepmother, who never cared very much for the children. A great famine had come over the land and there was barely a thing to eat.

With little food to go around, times were hard and the woodcutter's wife placed the blame on the children. The woman knew that if the children were no longer their concern, then she and her husband would have plenty to eat between them. She cooked up an evil plan to get rid of little Hansel and Gretel, once and for all.

Late one night, when the children were fast asleep in their beds, the woodcutter spoke of the troubles his family faced.

"I have thought and thought, and searched as much as any man could. There is no food to feed our little ones, not to mention ourselves," the woodcutter said, his brow furrowed with worry.

"Do not fret, my love. I have already come up with the perfect solution. The forest is rich with fruits and berries. We can leave the children there to live. There is no other way for all of us to survive."

"I only hope that you are right," the woodcutter said reluctantly.

"You needn't worry, my dear. I've thought it through well."

What the sinister woman had not realized was that the children had been nearby listening the whole time.

"Oh Gretel, what ever will we do?"

"Perhaps we could sneak back to the house once our stepmother has left. But how will we ever find our way back home?" Gretel asked with a worried tone.

The next afternoon, as Hansel and Gretel finished up their chores, their stepmother gathered them together for an outing in the forest—one to gather fruits and berries. They were each given a dry piece of bread to eat for their supper.

As the two children walked along through the forest, Hansel realized that he could break the bread into crumbs and leave a trail to lead them back home.

They gathered berries and grew quite tired with the work of the day. Their stepmother assured them that she would finish the work as they rested there for a little while. When Hansel and Gretel had settled into a deep sleep, their stepmother ran off, leaving them alone in the darkness of the forest.

Hansel and Gretel awoke to find themselves surrounded by the eerie sounds of night, and the moon shining brightly above them.

"Gretel! Let's go. We will just follow the trail of crumbs."

But when the children began to look for the trail that Hansel has left there was nothing to be found. The little creatures of the forest had eaten up all of the breadcrumbs. They were left with no way to get home.

Hansel and Gretel searched everywhere for the path, but it was no use. Each direction they turned looked the same as the last. After spending most of the night hopelessly wandering about, they snuggled together against the trunk of a grand tree.

As morning stretched over the forest, they awoke to the sound of a bird singing. They followed the song of the little bird, and it led them to the most magnificent house either of them had ever seen.

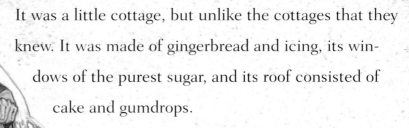

It was a little cottage, but unlike the cottages that they knew. It was made of gingerbread and icing, its windows of the purest sugar, and its roof consisted of cake and gumdrops.

"Food, Hansel! We've found food!" cried Gretel with much glee, as she broke a piece of the roof from its place and began to eat. Hansel, sharing in his sister's excitement, began to taste one of the windows.

From within the gingerbread walls came a quiet voice:

Nibbling, nibbling like a mouse

Who's that nibbling at my house?

The children were giddy with their discovery, and to the chant they replied:

We will not lie. We'll tell the truth

It's the wind that nibbles at your roof.

The children thought little of the voice and continued to feast on the sugary goodness of the house. Suddenly, the door of the cottage swung open and out stepped an ugly, old woman.

"Hello my children. Why are you here eating my humble little home?" asked the old woman.

"Please don't be angry," begged the children. "Our evil stepmother left us here in the forest to die. We've had nothing to eat and we're so very hungry. Please forgive us for eating your cottage."

The woman looked at the children with a toothless smile and said, "You children should join me inside for a bite to eat." Once they were inside, the children enjoyed all the milk and pancakes their bellies could hold. Once they were full, the old woman tucked them snugly into bed.

But as the children slept, the kind old woman who had helped them seemed to change. Her face grew mean and cold. For she wasn't a kind old woman at all, but rather an evil witch. And the evil witch loved nothing more than eating little children.

There she sat, watching her meal.

I think that I will eat the boy first, as the girl will take much more work.

She quietly scooped Hansel up from his warm comfortable spot, and locked him in a large cage that she kept hidden. Hansel screamed and yelled for Gretel to help him, but when Gretel awoke, Hansel was already behind the bars of the great cage.

"Yes, yes, get up, little one," said the evil witch to Gretel, "It is almost time that I feast on your brother. But first you shall fatten him up for me. Now, cook him something filling to eat!"

Without Hansel to help her, there was little that Gretel could do. And so, she obeyed the witch's commands, and spent the day feeding Hansel all that he could eat.

The witch would check, every so often, to see of Hansel was quite ready. "Give me your finger," the witch would say. But instead of his finger, Hansel would stick out a small twig that he had found at the bottom of the cage.

"Not any fatter! Not the tiniest bit fatter!" cried the witch. "Girl, you must make him more food! He is still far too thin to eat."

After many days had passed, the witch gave up on trying to fatten the boy.

"It has been long enough! I can wait no longer. It is time for your brother to be cooked." She instructed Gretel to check the temperature of the oven—it had to be hot enough.

Gretel looked over at the large oven and realized that the witch had yet another plan. As soon as Gretel crawled into the oven, the witch would push her in and slam the door shut. But Gretel was too smart to fall for the witch's trick.

"I do not know how to check the oven, ma'am."

"What do you mean, child? Simply crawl inside and check that the oven is quite hot enough!"

"I don't think that I will fit," said Gretel to
the witch.

"Of course you will fit," yelled the witch as she undid
her apron and stuck her head into the oven. Gretel wasted no time
and ran right up behind the witch and gave a great PUSH! She quickly
closed the oven door and locked it with a wooden spoon, slipped right
through the handles.

"Let me out of here! Let me out!" cried the witch. "I promise to never
eat any child ever again!"

But Gretel paid no attention to the witch's cries and went at once to
release her brother. Once Hansel was free, the two children ran outside,
happy to be away from that wicked witch.

But they still were unsure of which way to go. They heard the familiar
song of a little bird, and when they looked up, they found the same bird
that had led them to the cottage.

"Thank you, dear children. You have at last released me from the witch's evil spell, and I can once again fly free," said the bird. "Is there any way that I can repay you?"

"Can you take us home?" asked Gretel.

"Just follow me, and I will have you back home in no time at all."

When they reached their cottage, they found their father chopping wood, but there was no sign of their awful stepmother.

"Father, we're home!" cried the children.

"Oh, my dears! How happy I am to see you," exclaimed their father. "I have not slept a wink since you have been gone. I've missed you so much!"

He then told of how their stepmother had died during their time in the forest, and how he had been so all alone.

"But now, with my little Hansel and Gretel back home, life is good once again!"

And they all lived happily ever after.

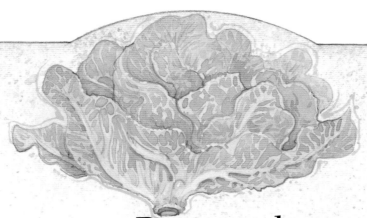

Rapunzel

Once upon a time, there was couple who lived in a simple but lovely home. Their upstairs window looked out over a magnificent garden. It flourished with delicious smelling herbs and delicate flowers. The garden's beauty did not at all reflect its keeper, as she was a horribly fierce witch.

The woman was with child, and would stand by the window and gaze upon the picturesque garden. She soon began to crave the wonderful rapunzel lettuce, which grew there. But as her craving became stronger, her body weakened with the knowledge that she would never partake of the evil witch's beautiful lettuce.

The man could not bear to see his wife suffer. It was not long before he ventured into the garden to take some of the lettuce and satisfy her craving. His wife was overjoyed and used the rapunzel to make a delightful salad. Unfortunately, the salad only increased her craving.

Her husband returned to the garden late one night to attain more of the greens for his wife. But as he attempted to leave the garden, the witch stepped out before him and cried, "No one steals from my garden! How dare you!"

The man pleaded for the witch's mercy and tried to explain what he had done. He told her of his wife's condition, and her need for the rapunzel lettuce. Hearing this, the witch spoke to the man.

"If what you say is true, then I will let you go, and you may take all of the rapunzel that your wife can eat. But you will pay with your first-born child."

Overwhelmed by fear, the man agreed and quickly returned home.

The day of the baby girl's birth, the witch appeared to claim her. She named her Rapunzel, for the lettuce that had ultimately brought the child to her.

Rapunzel grew into a exquisite child, with long, luxurious hair that resembled spun gold. It was in her twelfth year that the witch locked her in a lonely tower, deep within the forest. There was no way for Rapunzel to escape. The tower lacked any doors or stairs, and had but one small window that allowed her to see outside. When the witch came to see the girl she would stand beneath the window and cry:

"Rapunzel, Rapunzel, let down your golden hair."

Rapunzel would loosen her braids and lower her hair through the window. The witch would then climb it, like a ladder.

The years passed and Rapunzel remained a prisoner in the tower, her only visitor the witch. Then one afternoon a prince was passing through the forest and heard a lovely tune traveling in the air. He followed the sweet sound through the trees and found himself at the tower. The prince gazed upon the beautiful girl, but could see no way of reaching her. He returned each day just to listen to her sing.

One afternoon, as he listened to the Rapunzel's song, the prince spotted the witch. He watched as she went to the tower and called to the girl:

"Rapunzel, Rapunzel, let down your golden hair."

And as always, Rapunzel lowered her golden tresses and the witch climbed them.

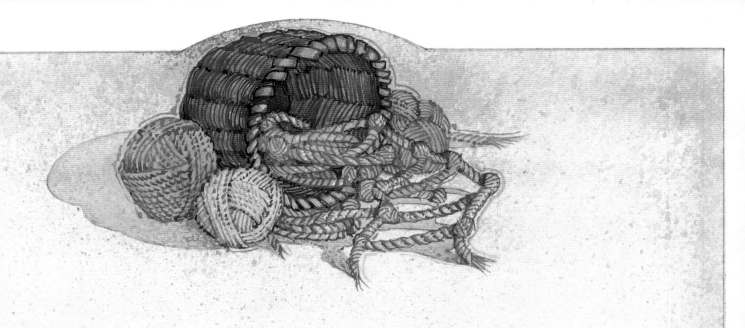

The next evening, the prince waited for the witch to leave, and then went to the tower. He cried out just as he had heard the witch:

"Rapunzel, Rapunzel, let down your golden hair."

The golden hair tumbled down as it always had with the witch, and the prince used it to climb to the top of the tower. Rapunzel was startled at the appearance of the stranger. She had never before seen a man. But he soon won her trust with his gentle nature. He visited her often and eventually asked her to marry him, and Rapunzel accepted.

Together, they developed a plan for her escape from the tower and the witch. Upon each visit to Rapunzel, the prince would bring her a skein of silk. She would weave the silk into a ladder and when it was completed, would climb down from the tower and be with her handsome prince.

The witch had not known of the prince and his many visits to the tower. Until, one day, without thinking, Rapunzel asked the witch why the prince was able to climb up her hair far more quickly than she.

Anger flooded the face of the witch and she yelled as she never had before.

"I have kept you here, safe from the rest of the world. You have lied to me, you awful child!"

The witch swept across the room and cut off Rapunzel's beautiful hair. She then banished her to a barren land, where the girl lived in misery.

It was in the same day that the witch planned to catch the prince. She took the braids that she had cut from Rapunzel's hair, and hung them from the tower's window. The prince climbed the golden hair, just as he always had. But when he reached the top of the tower, he was met by the evil witch.

"Your love is no longer here. She has gone to another place and you shall never see her again!"

So distraught was the prince by the witch's words that he jumped from the tower. He landed in a thorn bush and his life was spared. But the thorns damaged his eyes horribly, and he could no longer see.

The years passed and the prince wandered about aimlessly, only able to think of his lost love . . . Rapunzel. One day, without realizing it, the prince roamed into the very desert where Rapunzel had been sent to live.

The prince soon heard a familiar sound, a lovely song, and again he followed it. At the very sight of the prince, Rapunzel let out a great cry. She ran to him and wrapped him in her arms. The tears of joy that she wept fell upon his eyes and his sight was restored.

The prince, at long last, returned to his kingdom with Rapunzel, where they lived out their days in great joy and happiness.

The Old Woman
in the Forest

A long time ago there was a peasant girl who found herself lost in the forest. She broke down into tears, and asked, "Whatever will I do? I shall never be able to find my way out of this forest. I will surely starve to death."

She searched and searched for a way out, but there was none to be found. As night fell, she found a tree under which she planned to sit, regardless of what might happen around her. Suddenly, a small white dove flew to her, clasping a golden key in its beak. It placed the key in her delicate hand and began to speak. "In that large tree over there, you will find a small door with a lock on it. Open it with this key and you will find all the food and drink that you need. You will not have to go hungry any longer."

She followed the instructions of the little dove and within the tree she found enough milk and bread to keep her from ever becoming hungry again. After eating to her heart's content, she said, " I'm so very tired. I wish that I could lie in my bed and rest."

Again, the dove flew by and, carrying another golden key directed her to another tree. Within the tree she found a soft, lovely bed where she was able to find comfort and sleep. Upon her waking, she was led to another tree where she found clothing lined with jewels and gold, grander even than those of a princess.

And so she went on for some time, the dove caring for all of her needs as they arose, and she was happy.

One day the dove came to her asking for a favor in return. The maiden said that she would gladly do anything that she could, as he had done so very much for her.

The dove began to instruct her and the maiden listened carefully. "I will lead you to a small cottage, and there you will find an old woman seated by the hearth. She will greet you, but you are not to answer her. Go right by her and you will come to a door. Open it and you will find many rings, magnificent ones, with glistening stones, but you are to leave them alone. Find the simple one among them and bring it to me as quickly as you can."

The maiden found her way to the old woman's cottage and as she entered was greeted just as the dove had said would happen. She did not answer and went directly to the door.

"Where are you going?" cried the woman. "This is my cottage and no one may enter without my permission." She grabbed at the maiden's skirt, but was unable to keep a hold of her. The maiden entered the room beyond the door and found a grand selection of rings lying before her. They were glimmering and more beautiful than she could have imagined. While she was searching for the simple ring that the dove had described she noticed that the old woman was lurking nearby with a birdcage in her hand. The maiden approached the woman and took the birdcage from her. As she lifted it and looked inside, she discovered a bird with a simple ring clasped in its beak. She took the ring and ran off as quickly as she could.

She waited for the dove, certain that it would come to her to collect the ring. As she waited, she leaned against a tree and felt as its branches became soft and comforting. Soon, the tree seemed to be embracing her, its branches gently wrapped around her. She turned to look, but there was no longer a tree, but a handsome man who pulled her close and kissed her sweetly.

"Oh, dear maiden! You have saved me from the powers of that wicked witch! She had cast an evil spell on me, which had turned me to a tree, unable to move or speak. For a short time each day, I was transformed into a dove. I could fly about and sing a song, but still, I was not free from her, not as long as she was the holder of the ring. I feared that I might never be human again."

Tree after tree in the forest began to change, revealing numerous horses and servants. For the man that the maiden had saved was a prince of great wealth and fortune. They traveled to his kingdom, where they married and lived happily ever after.

Brier Rose

In days long past, there was a couple, a king and queen, who spent each day in their magnificent palace wishing for only one thing, a child. Years came and went, and yet they were never blessed with a child.

A frog appeared to the queen as she was bathing one day. He came to her and said, "The wish of the great king and queen shall be granted. In the year to come, you shall bear a daughter."

The queen thought little of what the frog had said, as she was sure that she would never have a child. But the frog had spoken the truth and within the year, the people of the kingdom were celebrating the birth of the king and queen's daughter, the princess. The king and queen were so elated at the arrival of the child that they decided to hold a grand feast to celebrate. They invited what seemed to be the whole of the kingdom. This included thirteen wise women. Unfortunately, there were only twelve golden plates from which they could eat. Therefore, one of them would be unable to attend.

The feast was celebrated with great jubilation, and as it was nearing the end, the twelve wise women came forward to bequeath their gifts to the infant princess. She was given such gifts as beauty, wealth, and virtue. As the twelfth wise woman was about to give the child her gift, the thirteenth woman, who had not been included in the celebration, burst into the room, seeking revenge. The evil woman hovered over the child and placed an evil curse upon her, "Upon the dawning of her fifteenth year, the princess shall prick her finger on a spindle and die!"

With that, she turned and left all of
the people of the kingdom standing
there in horrified silence. The twelfth
wise woman stepped forward to give the
child her gift. While she did not have
the power to undo the evil curse, she could
change the outcome.

"Upon pricking her finger on the
spindle, the princess shall fall into a peace-
ful slumber of one hundred years, but
will not die."

The king was still not satisfied and
was determined to do all that he could to
protect his precious daughter. All spindles
in the kingdom were ordered destroyed by
him, and he watched over the years as his
daughter grew into a beautiful young woman. Each of
the gifts of the wise women were apparent in the kind and
gentle ways of the princess.

On the day of her fifteenth birthday, the princess found herself
alone in the palace, the king and queen away for the day. And so
the princess explored the many rooms and chambers of the
palace that she had never before seen. She soon came to
the tower, and climbed to the top of a tall, winding
staircase that ended at a small door. She unlocked
the door with a key that sat in the rusty
lock, and found a simple old woman,
spinning flax upon a spindle.

"What is that you are doing?" she questioned the old woman.

"Why, I'm spinning."

"What is that?" asked the princess, as she reached out and touched the bobbing spindle. And with that, the princess fell upon the bed that sat beside her, in a deep, deep sleep. It did not take long before this silent slumber had reached the rest of the kingdom. The king and the queen, the horses in the stables, the birds of the sky, all fell into the same deep sleep as the princess. All became quiet and still. There were no fires or winds— no sound or tremble.

A brier hedge began to grow all along the walls of the great castle, and it soon covered so great an area that the palace could no longer be seen. The princess became known as the beautiful sleeping Brier Rose, and her story was passed from town to town and country to country. Many princes came with the hopes of saving the princess and winning her heart. But the brier hedge was far too strong and treacherous to get through.

Many years had passed since the curse had fallen upon the kingdom, when a prince came to the country and heard the tale of the beautiful princess, asleep within the brier-covered walls of the castle. Many tried to warn the prince against trying to save the princess. No man had ever made it past the thorns of the brier. But the young prince showed no fear, and set out to save the beautiful Brier Rose.

It was on the last day of the hundredth year of her slumber that the prince set forth to save the princess. As the prince approached the palace, he found beautiful blossoms in the place of the brier's menacing thorns. He walked easily through its gates, only to find the entire kingdom fast asleep. As he looked around, he could see everyone from the king's cook to the fly on the wall sleeping peacefully. Still, he did not see the princess.

After much searching, he came to the tower. He climbed the staircase and opened the door, and there was the princess. She lay silently on the same bed that had held her for one hundred years. Her beauty was so overwhelming that the prince could not bear to take his eyes off of her for even a moment. He walked to her bedside, leaned down, and placed a gentle kiss upon her lips. Slowly, Brier Rose's eyes opened and she was freed from the curse.

Together, they walked down from the tower and looked around the palace. All around, the kingdom was waking from its extended rest. Soon, the horses, the hounds, the pigeons, and even the flies on the wall were awake.

Brier Rose and the handsome prince soon wed, and were celebrated with much joy. Together, they lived happily for all the days of their lives.

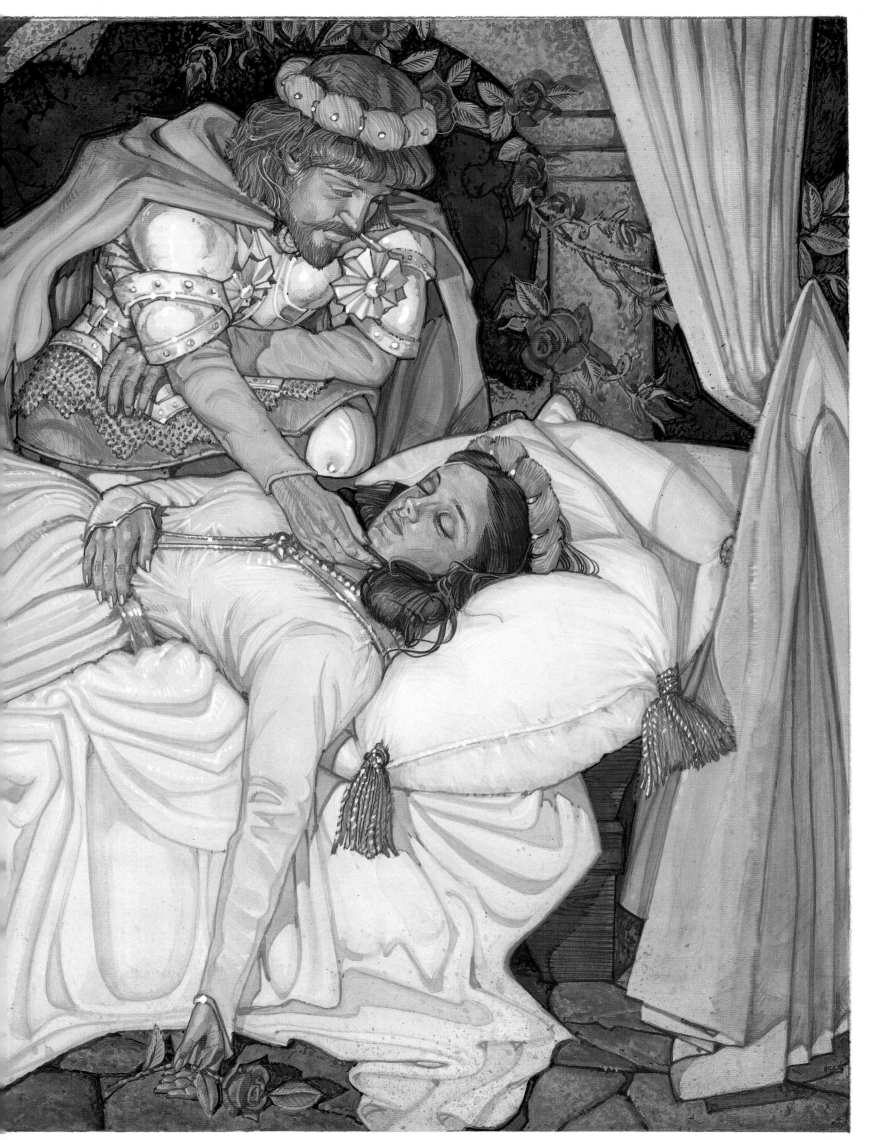